MW01102116

THE STORM WIFE

Retold by BOB BARTON   Illustrated by GEORGI YUDIN

QUARRY PRESS

Long ago in the cold snowy lands beneath the Northern Lights there lived an old man who had three daughters. Once a terrible snowstorm blew

down on the tundra. For three
days and three nights the people
huddled in their tents cold,
hungry, and too frightened to
poke their noses out of doors.

"Kotura the Wind Giant is angry," said the old man to his daughters. "His one and only wish is to take from us a wife wise in the ways of her people. Eldest Daughter, you must go to Kotura. Ask him to halt the storm or our people will surely die."

"How can I go to him?" she asked. "I don't know the way."

"I will tell you," replied the old man. "Take our sled and face it into the wind. Give it a push and follow it. The wind will tear open the strings of your coat; do not pause to tie them. Snow will fill your boots; do not shake it out. Never stop until you reach a tall mountain. Climb it. When you reach the top, tie the strings of your coat, shake the snow from your boots, jump onto the sled, and coast down the mountain. You will stop beside a large tent. This is Kotura's dwelling place. Enter, but touch nothing. When Kotura comes, mind and do as he bids you."

Eldest Daughter pulled on her coat and boots, faced the sled into the wind, and with a push sent it gliding along. As she ran, the wind blew hard, her coat flew open, and snow filled her boots. "If I wait until I reach the mountain to tie up my coat and empty my boots, I'll freeze," she thought. "I'll do it now." She continued her journey pushing into the wind, walking, and walking, until at last she reached a mountain. She climbed the mountain.

At the top a tiny bird
floundered in a deep drift,
unable to free its wings
from the snow. Eldest Daughter,
impatient to be off, pretended not
to see it. She jumped onto the sled and
plunged down, down, then glided up to
a large tent. Eldest Daughter stepped
inside, looked around, and saw meat
simmering in a pot. She built up the fire to
warm herself, tore a strip from the meat,
and ate it. It was so delicious that she tore off
another and another until she had eaten her fill.

A sudden gust of wind shook the tent. The skin that hung over the entrance was raised and a giant entered. It was Kotura. "Who are you?" he demanded. "What are you doing in my tent?"

"My father sent me. I have come to be your wife."

Kotura turned to the fire. He took some meat from the pot, piled it on a wooden platter, and said, "Take this to the neighboring tent. An old woman will come out to you. Give her the meat, but do not go in. Wait until she returns the platter."

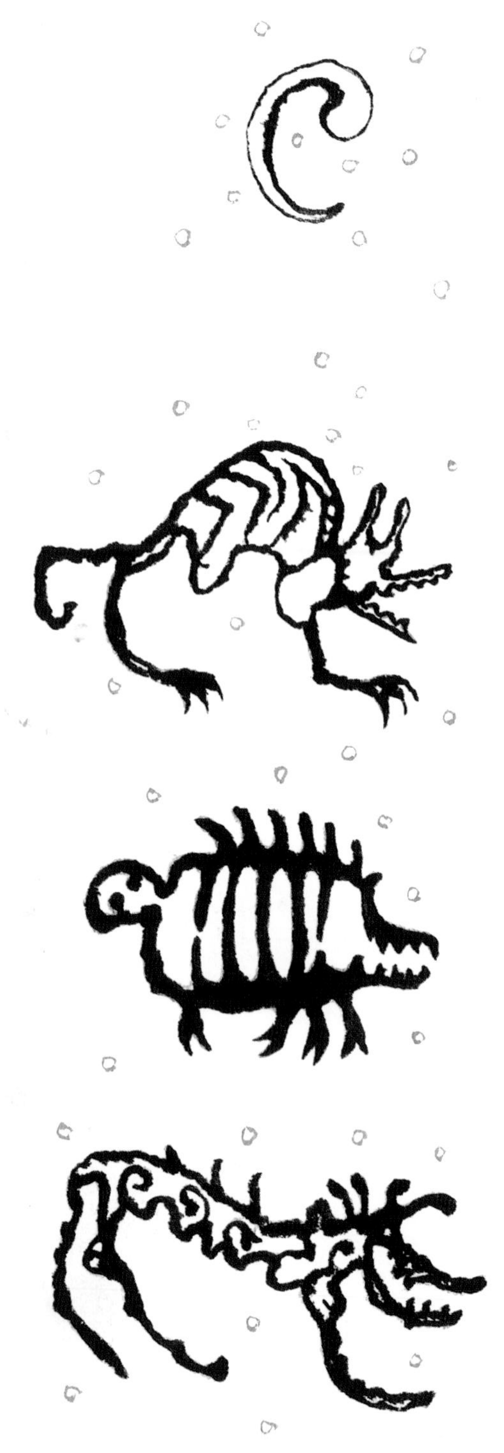

Eldest daughter took the meat and went outside. Thick driving snow flew into her face. "How am I to find my way in this storm?" she cried. She stumbled about aimlessly, then threw the meat into the snow. When she returned to Kotura's tent, the giant glanced at the empty platter.

"Were you given anything in return for the meat?"

She shook her head, no.

Kotura went to bed.

In the morning Kotura shook Eldest Daughter awake. "I am going hunting," he said. "While I am gone, fetch one of those skins from the pile in the corner. Dress it and make me a coat by evening." Then he left.

Eldest Daughter rose and seized a skin from the pile. Hurriedly she dressed and cut it. Suddenly the skin hanging over the entrance was raised and an old woman entered. "Child," she pleaded, "there is a mote in my eye. Please help me!"

"Can't you see I'm busy?" snapped Eldest Daughter. "Find someone else."

The old woman shuffled quietly out. Eldest Daughter rushed ahead with the work. She rushed so much that the edges were ragged, the sides uneven, and the stitches too far apart. In the evening Kotura returned. "Have you finished the coat?" he asked.

Eldest Daughter handed it to him. Kotura ran his hand over it. It was badly dressed and felt rough to the touch. He saw that the garment was poorly cut and that the stitches would not hold. What was worse, it did not fit. Kotura threw back his head and shrieked his displeasure. The tent pitched from side to side. A strong wind raced through the entrance, lifted Eldest Daughter off her feet, and hurled her into the storm.

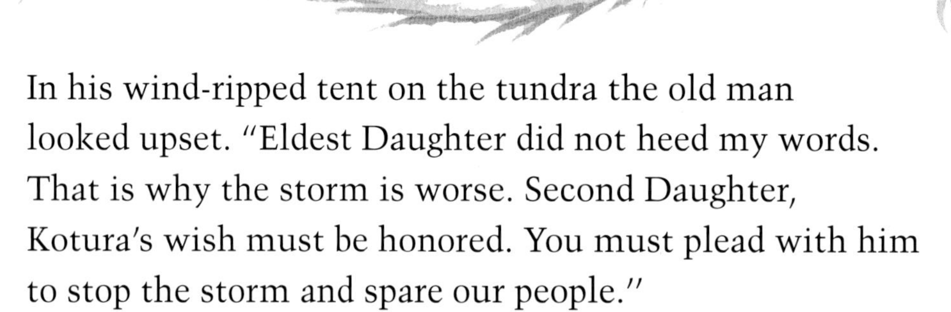

In his wind-ripped tent on the tundra the old man looked upset. "Eldest Daughter did not heed my words. That is why the storm is worse. Second Daughter, Kotura's wish must be honored. You must plead with him to stop the storm and spare our people."

The old man made a sled of antler and bones. Then he told her what he had told Eldest Daughter. "Go now and do as I say."

Second Daughter faced the sled into the wind and, giving it a push, ran along behind. The strings of her coat flew apart. Her boots filled with snow. She beat her arms against her sides and struggled on.

On the mountaintop, as she tied her coat and shook the snow from her boots, she spied the tiny bird half frozen in the snow. She reached out and knocked the snow from its wings but did not wait to see if it could fly.

She jumped onto the sled, plummeted down the mountainside, and when she reached the Wind Giant's tent, she entered and helped herself to his food. Soon Kotura returned and saw her.

"Why have you come to me?"

"My father sent me to be your wife," she replied.

Kotura turned to the fire. He reached into the cooking pot and heaped meat onto a wooden platter. "Carry this to my neighbor but do not enter the dwelling. Remain outside until the platter has been passed back to you."

Second Daughter took the meat and went outside. For awhile she wandered in the snow and biting wind, then she shook her fist at the tent and declared angrily, "I'll go no farther." She threw the meat into the snow, then stood a while. Finally she went back in.

"You have come back very soon. Did you deliver the meat? Show me the platter." Second Daughter held out the empty platter. Kotura looked at it, then went to bed.

In the morning he shook Second Daughter awake, pointed to a pile of skins in the corner, and ordered her to make a coat for him by evening. Second Daughter grabbed a skin and hastily set to work.

Suddenly an old woman entered the tent. "A mote has got into my eye, child," she said. "I cannot seem to get it out."

"Go away," screamed Second Daughter. "I have work to do."

The old woman said nothing and went away. Second Daughter worked quickly and carelessly. Sleeve lengths did not match, seams ran all askew. When Kotura came back that evening and saw the garment, his wails of disappointment rocked the tent and sent Second Daughter whirling into the teeth of the storm.

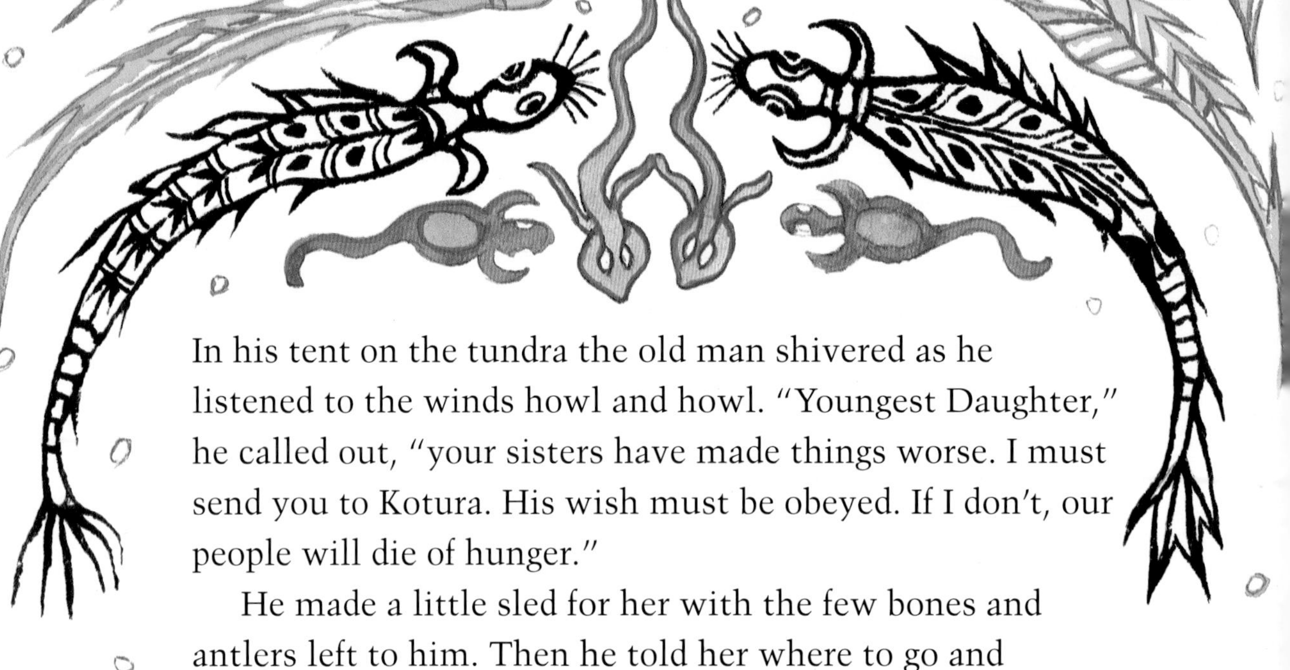

In his tent on the tundra the old man shivered as he listened to the winds howl and howl. "Youngest Daughter," he called out, "your sisters have made things worse. I must send you to Kotura. His wish must be obeyed. If I don't, our people will die of hunger."

He made a little sled for her with the few bones and antlers left to him. Then he told her where to go and what to do.

Youngest Daughter stepped into the icy blast and gave the sled a push. As she followed, snow filled her boots and the strings of her coat were blown apart. On and on she plodded, remembering not to stop. When she reached the mountaintop, she paused. As she was shaking the snow from her boots, she saw the tiny bird half buried in the drifts. She freed it from the snow and stroked its feathers gently. Then the bird flew off and Youngest Daughter climbed onto the sled, coasted down the mountain, and stopped in front of Kotura's tent.

She went in and stood waiting. Meat simmered in a pot over the fire, but she did not touch it. The skins over the entrance parted and Kotura swept in on a blast of cold air.

"Why are you here?" he asked.

"My father sent me to plead for my people. They are cold and starving. They will die if you do not stop the storm."

"Build up the fire and we'll eat some meat," he said. "I'm hungry and you must be also. I can see that you've eaten nothing."

Youngest Daughter took the meat from the pot and gave it to the giant.

When they had eaten, he put meat on a wooden platter and told her to take it to the neighboring tent and wait. Youngest Daughter took the platter and stepped out into the blizzard. She peered into the swirling whiteness. The wind howled in her ears. She had no idea where to go. Something flew at her face. It was the tiny bird from the mountaintop. It darted towards her, flew away, then circled back.

"I will follow the bird," she thought. Where the bird went, she went. Then she saw sparks flashing and came upon a large mound. Smoke was curling from the top of it. She walked around looking for an entrance. Suddenly the side of the mound opened and an old woman looked out.

"Whatever are you doing here?" she cried.

"Kotura sent this meat for you."

"Kotura you say? Very well then, let me have it and wait here."

Youngest Daughter stood by the mound and waited for a long time. After awhile the side of the mound opened again and the old woman handed back the platter. There was something on it, but Youngest Daughter couldn't see what it was. She returned to Kotura's tent.

"Have you delivered the meat?"

"I have," she replied.

"Show me the plate."

Kotura could see that it was piled with knives and steel needles and scrapers and brakes for dressing skins. "You have received many fine things that will come in handy for you," he laughed.

In the morning Kotura brought a pile of skins to Youngest Daughter. "I want you to make me a coat by evening. If it is made well, I will help you," he said, and left the tent.

Youngest Daughter sorted carefully through the skins. Several she pulled over her shoulders to try for size. When she found the right one, she fetched the wooden platter. There was everything she needed to make a coat. She placed the needles and knives on her lap and thought to herself, "How much can I do in only one day?"

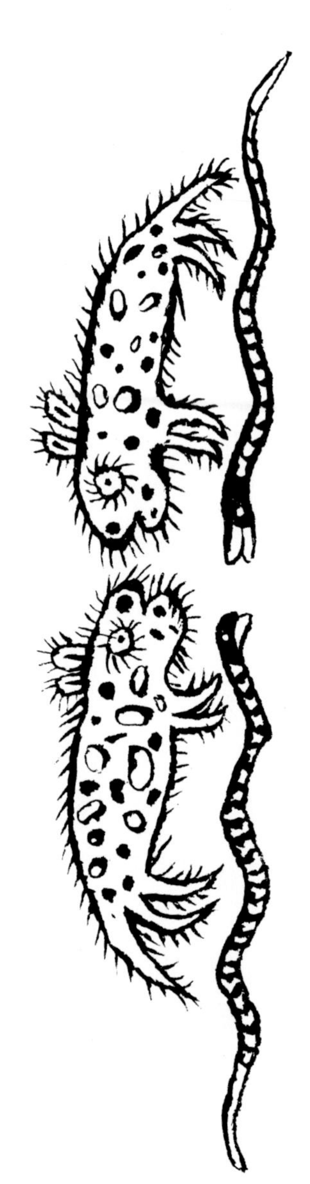

Just then the skin over the entrance was lifted and an old woman entered. "Help me child! There is a mote in my eye. Please take it out for me!"

Youngest Daughter recognized the old woman from the night before. Quickly she removed the dust particle from the old woman's eye. "That is so much better," sighed the old woman. "My eye doesn't hurt any more. Come closer child and look in my right ear," she chuckled. Youngest Daughter looked into the old woman's ear and squealed, "There's a girl sitting in your ear!"

"Call her out," urged the old woman. "She'll help you make Kotura's coat."

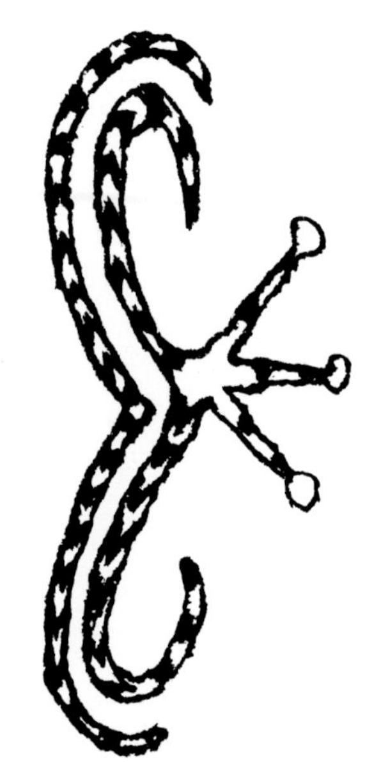

Youngest Daughter was overjoyed. She called to the girl. Not one, but four girls jumped out of the old woman's ear, nodding and smiling. They set to work and helped Youngest Daughter dress and scrape skins, then they helped with the cutting and sewing. In no time, the coat was ready. It was beautiful. The four girls jumped back into the old woman's ear, and she went away.

Kotura returned in the evening and asked to see the coat. Youngest Daughter handed it to him. He passed his hand over the surface. "This feels very soft, very pleasant to the touch." Next he tried it on. It was not too large and not too small.

"Not only does it fit me, it is beautiful," he exclaimed. Then Kotura smiled. "Youngest Daughter, I like you. My mother likes you too! And so do my four sisters! You have courage and you work well. You braved the storm so that your people might not die. Please do not leave us. Be my bride and stay with me."

As he spoke these words, the storm on the tundra was stilled and the people one and all came out of their tents into the light of day.

*For
Doreen*

The Storm Wife is adapted from a Nenets folktale entitled "Kotura, Lord of the Winds," in *Northern Lights: Fairy Tales of the Peoples of the North* (Progress Press, Moscow, 1976).

The publisher gratefully acknowledges the assistance of The Canada Council, the Ontario Arts Council, the Department of Communications, and the Ontario Publishing Centre.

Special thanks to Dmitrij Khachaturian of Progress Publishers in Moscow for his work as agent for Georgi Yudin, as well as Diane Dawber, Lissa Paul, Diane Wolkstein, and David Booth.

Canadian Cataloguing in Publication Data
Barton, Robert, 1939-
The Storm Wife
(Classic folktale series)
ISBN 1-55082-060-5 (bound) -
ISBN 1-55082-061-3 (pbk.)
I. Yudin, Georgi II. Title. III. Series
PS8553.A7807S76 1993 398'.2
C93-090072-3 PZ8.1.B37St 1993

Graphic Design: Peter Dorn RCA, FGDC
Printed in Hong Kong by Everbest
Published by Quarry Press, Inc.
P.O. Box 1061, Kingston, Ontario K7L 4Y5